Drive Thru

by Erica David

Illustrated by Robert Dress

SCHOLASTIC INC.

New York   Toronto   London   Auckland   Sydney
Mexico City   New Delhi   Hong Kong   Buenos Aires

Published by Scholastic Inc.,
90 Old Sherman Turnpike, Danbury, Connecticut 06816.

SCHOLASTIC and associated logos are trademarks
and/or registered trademarks of Scholastic Inc.

ISBN 0-439-56316-X

First Scholastic Printing, August 2004

Chapters

SQUEAK
SQUEAK
SQUEAK

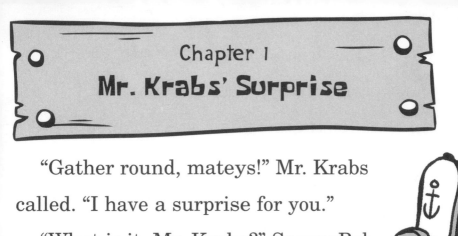

Chapter 1
Mr. Krabs' Surprise

"Gather round, mateys!" Mr. Krabs called. "I have a surprise for you."

"What is it, Mr. Krabs?" SpongeBob SquarePants eagerly asked.

"It's me dream come true," Mr. Krabs answered. "A drive-through window! And just in time for the Eels on Wheels convention!"

"Oh, joy," Squidward Tentacles said dryly.

"Mr. Squidward, I think you're missing the importance of this innovation," suggested Mr. Krabs.

"It's possible," Squidward replied.

11

"For years now, the Krusty Krab has been serving delicious Krabby Patties to the citizens of Bikini Bottom," Mr. Krabs explained. "It's our job to feed as many hungry people as we can."

"Not just our job, it's our duty," SpongeBob agreed.

"Right you are, lad," said Mr. Krabs.

"With this little beauty, we'll be able to serve more customers in less time! And the best part is, they don't even have to leave the comfort of their boats!" Mr. Krabs finished.

"That's wonderful, sir!" exclaimed SpongeBob.

"Very moving," Squidward said dully. "But who's going to work this drive through?"

TAP
TAP
TAP

"Why, you and SpongeBob, of course,"
Mr. Krabs replied.

"But we're already busy with the
customers inside the restaurant,"
Squidward complained.

"C'mon, Squidward, we can do it!"
SpongeBob cried. "I-I-I'm READY!"

"That's the spirit, SpongeBob, me boy!" said Mr. Krabs, chuckling. "All hands on deck! It's going to be a busy day!"

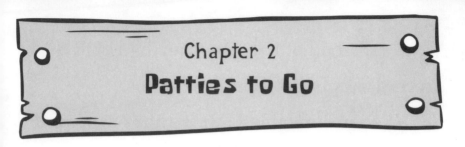

The new drive through at the Krusty Krab was an immediate success. There were so many customers that SpongeBob and Squidward could barely keep up with all of the orders.

By the end of the day, they had sold a record number of Krabby Patties.

"It's unbelievable!" Mr. Krabs exclaimed. "Business has nearly tripled!"

"Is it closing time yet?" Squidward whined.

"I could go on cooking all night!" SpongeBob said brightly. "But sadly, it's time to go home."

"Good work, lads," Mr. Krabs congratulated them. "I'm gonna be rich— I mean, wasn't this a rich experience?"

"Um, Mr. Krabs?" SpongeBob asked.

SQUEAK
SQUEAK
SQUEAK

"Do you think that tomorrow maybe I could work at the window?"

"Oh, please let him work at the window!" Squidward begged.

"Now SpongeBob," Mr. Krabs replied.
"You're me ace fry cook. Your place is in
the kitchen."

"But, Mr. Krabs—" SpongeBob cried.

"But, nothing. You're not to touch this headset. Understood?" said Mr. Krabs sternly. SpongeBob nodded sadly.

"Good," said Mr. Krabs. "Well, SpongeBob, it's your turn to clean and lock up. I'll see you both bright and early tomorrow morning."

SpongeBob was busy mopping the floor

when he heard a voice call from outside:

"Hey, SpongeBob,

I'm here to pick you

up from work!"

"Okay, Patrick, I'm almost finished," SpongeBob told his friend Patrick Star.

"Uh, SpongeBob," Patrick said, "there's a new, funny-looking window attached to the Krusty Krab."

"I know, Pat. It's the new drive through,"
SpongeBob replied, as he slid open the window.

Patrick fell into the room. "Oooo . . . drive
through. How's it work?" asked Patrick.

SpongeBob patiently explained to his friend.

"You mean you get to wear this cool head thingy and lean out of the window all day?" Patrick wondered.

"Not exactly," SpongeBob answered. "That's Squidward's job."

"But it's so shiny! Look, there are buttons on it and everything!" Patrick pointed out.

"No, Pat! Mr. Krabs said I can't touch the headset," said SpongeBob firmly.

"Okay, but it would look really good on you, SpongeBob," Patrick gushed.

"I can't, Patrick." SpongeBob shook his head.

"Touch it," whispered Patrick. "Go on, *touch it.*"

"Must . . . not . . . touch . . . the . . . ," SpongeBob murmured weakly.

"Put it on, SpongeBob! Put it on!"
Patrick shouted.

SpongeBob couldn't resist any longer!
He yanked the headset onto his head.

"Now push the buttons!" Patrick cried.

SpongeBob jabbed at the buttons.

"Welcome to the Krusty Krab!" he roared.

"Can I take your order?"

"You're open late? Awesome!" said a voice. "I'll have a Krabby Patty Supreme."

"There's a customer! Ooooo, I'm in trouble!" SpongeBob whispered in horror. "What am I going to do?"

"I dunno." Patrick shrugged. "*You* work here."

"You're right, Patrick, I do, and it's my job—no, my *duty*—to feed the hungry," SpongeBob said. "Let's get to work!"

Moments later, SpongeBob handed a piping-hot Krabby Patty through the window. "Thank you, sir," he said. "Come again!"

The customer drove off.

"Another job well done," SpongeBob said with a sigh. He reached up to take off the headset.

"Hey, buddy!" called a gruff voice through the earpiece. "Are you gonna take my order or what?"

SpongeBob leaned out of the window. "Oh no!" he cried. "The Eels on Wheels convention!"

SpongeBob and Patrick scrambled to fill as many orders as they could, but the line of eels just kept growing.

"How many customers have we served?" SpongeBob asked breathlessly.

"Uh, three . . . I think," Patrick answered.

"Three? But I cooked at least 50 Krabby Patties!" SpongeBob exclaimed.

"PATRICK!" screamed SpongeBob. "You've been eating the patties!"

"I was weak with hunger. This is hard work," Patrick mumbled through a mouthful of food.

"But the patties are for the customers!" SpongeBob cried.

"Sorry, SpongeBob," Patrick apologized.

"Hey! Where's my food?" one of the customers yelled.

"Yeah, we've been waiting 20 minutes!" another shouted.

"Uh-oh, SpongeBob," said Patrick. "I think they're angry."

"KRAB-BY PAT-TY! KRAB-BY PAT-TY!"

the crowd at the drive through began to chant.

"We're hungry!" screamed one of the eels.

"And we don't like being hungry,

do we, boys?"

The mob responded in angry agreement.

"This doesn't sound good,"

SpongeBob whispered.

"KRAB-BY PAT-TY! KRAB-BY PAT-TY!"

the angry mob continued to chant.

Chapter 5
SpongeBob GeniusPants

Meanwhile, Mr. Krabs was dreaming in his hammock.

"What's that, SpongeBob?" he muttered. "You lost me lucky dollar?"

"KRAB-BY PAT-TY! KRAB-BY PAT-TY!"

Mr. Krabs popped awake at the
distant sound.

"Why, someone's calling for me Krabby
Patties!" he exclaimed.

Mr. Krabs ran to the window.

"Why is there a crowd at the Krusty Krab?" he wondered. "I'd better get down there!"

Mr. Krabs arrived at the restaurant just in time. The angry mob had poured inside, and SpongeBob and Patrick were surrounded.

"What in blazes is going on here?"
Mr. Krabs demanded.

"Mr. Krabs!" SpongeBob cried.

"SpongeBob! I should've known!" Mr.
Krabs bellowed. Then he turned to the eel
leader. "And you! Who do you think you are
bargin' into me restaurant?"

"Uh, sorry, sir, but that nervous sponge took way too long with our orders," the eel leader said sheepishly.

"I'm sooo sorry, Mr. Krabs!" SpongeBob sobbed. "I'm not fit to wear this uniform! I've betrayed you and fry cooks everywhere—"

"Get up!" Mr. Krabs interrupted. "You're a genius, SpongeBob!"

"What?" SpongeBob asked, puzzled.

"Keeping the drive through open late is brilliant!" said Mr. Krabs. "Think of the money to be made!"

"You mean, I'm not fired?" said SpongeBob timidly.

"Of course not! I'll be taking the cost of any damage out of your paycheck, but I couldn't fire me number-one fry cook," Mr. Krabs assured him.

"Oh, thank you!" SpongeBob cried.

"Now get back in the kitchen and make
these fine gentlemen some Krabby Patties!"
Mr. Krabs ordered.

"Aye-aye, sir!" SpongeBob answered, as he dashed into the kitchen.

"Argghhh!" said Mr. Krabs to himself. "This gives me an idea!"

TWO WEEKS LATER...

"Oh, Mr. Krabs," SpongeBob exclaimed.
"I can't believe you're letting me cook *AND*
work at the window. I don't deserve this!"

"*I* don't deserve *this!*" Squidward wailed.